For Sister Johnymae!

Love you 4ever!

Love and Peace Always

We dedicate this book to our great-great grandmother who cleverly eluded slave catchers and endured life in a hidden cave.

You have taught us to always cherish freedom.

Cathi Wright Jewel

10/10/16

Published by Cathie Wright-Lewis
Cover Art , Book Design & Illustrations by Cheyenne Angel Lewis
Information available at: www.cathiewrightlewis.com
ISBN: 978-1537512075

Every 33 years, the Leonid Meteor
Showers rocket, then burst
across the night sky.
It's the perfect time for Mama
Relly to take a ride.

She sails on the tail with one
thing on her mind,
She has a story to tell and
kinfolk to find...

*"She appeared out of thin air,
that cold, dark night when I expected snow...
Like a falling star, she burst on sight...
How? I'll never know..."*

"Just 5 more minutes, ... please! Sherry and I had begged Mama before bedtime one cold November night.

"No way girls," Mama whispered. The sound of Dad opening the front door meant it was past our bedtime. We tippy-toed backwards to the staircase trying to glimpse at our favorite tv show when Sam the Weatherman interrupted the show with the best news an eight year-old like me could hear.

"Here's a forecast you kids are going to love!"

We all froze like ice pops and glared at the screen.

"Our first storm of the 1998 season is on the way. It promises a foot of fluffy flakes and the possibility of a, ... snow day!" Mr. Weatherman sang like we had just won a prize on game show.

"YES!" I screamed and threw my arms in the air like I had won the World Series. My little sister Sherry joined me.

Together we jumped up and down like kangaroos across the living room floor. We gave one another high-fives each time we passed each other around Mama's mahogany and marble coffee table.

"Watch those corners girls," Mama warned. She chuckled as we made our last leg around the table and hopped up the stairs to our bedroom. Like Sherry, I should've been pooped from all of that jumping and hopped right into bed but like most snow day lovers, I was too excited to sleep.

"Get in that bed now, Cyndi!" Mama fussed then pointed at my bed, "Sam the Weatherman didn't say a thing about schools being closed tomorrow. He just said the snow is 'on the 'way'. So don't get too excited," she said with a raised eyebrow.

She watched me hop on my bed and under my mud cloth quilt. "But I know you, ..." she moved in close enough to poke and tickle my belly, "That's not gonna keep you from wishing for it though."

She had already moved over to Sherry's bed and kissed her sleeping forehead before I could stop laughing and respond. The bright hall light faded with her laugh as she closed my bedroom door and blew me a goodnight kiss.

"He said possible!" I yelled and blew one back. I pretended to close my eyes and listened for Mama's footsteps to make creaking sounds down the staircase.

Ever so lightly, I crept out of bed. On tippy-toes, I rushed to the window over Sherry's bed. I pounced on her then bounced to my knees to accidentally wake her up, on purpose. But Sherry was out like a light.

Shaking Sherry's bed as hard as I could only made her whine in her sleep, "Stop Cynd-eee! Go - to – bed," she grumbled with closed eyes and turned over.

I laid my head on her pillow to make sure she could hear me, "Mama's gone Sherry. Wake up!" I whispered as loud as I could directly in her ear.

"Mmm, … mmm," her long, loud snore sounded like she just took a bite of Daddy's famous red velvet cake, paused as it melted down her throat then licked her lips. It also told me to forget about her joining me at the window to snow-watch.

"You're gonna miss everything, sleepyhead," I warned and turned to gaze at the white dust sprinkling from the moon-less sky.

I rested my face between my cupped hands planted on the ledge. Hypnotized, I watched.

I had glued myself to the windowsill for hours, and slipped in and out of dreams as I waited for snow. My head nodded and popped up like a bobble head doll. Nod and pop.

Nod and pop. Around the third nod, I heard a sizzle before the pop. Sizzle? I wondered... What's that sizzle?

To push the sleep away, I stretched my eyes as wide as saucers; stretched my neck too. Before I could search for the sizzle, tiny drizzling snowflakes turned into a shower of firecrackers.

The sky became an exploding rainbow filled with colorful falling stars. Like sparkling fireworks, they formed a swirling circle that exploded from every possible direction like a sparkling pinwheel.

Over and over, they burst before my face on the window and the outside windowsill too. I laughed as they snapped, crackled and popped like Rice Krispies Cereal.

"Sherry!!" I yelled and shook the bed with my knees again, "I think it's snowing fire! And look, a huge comet is dropping out of the sky!"

"Mmm, … mmm," said Sherry when I looked down at her, hoping I was loud enough to wake her.

" On the tail of the comet
and amongst the stars,
a beautiful brown lady flies,
From a different place and a different
time, she brings a great surprise. "

Scared and shook, I dove under her covers and buried my head under Sherry's pillow, "Please wake up Sherry," I cried. "Something's coming!"

But the seven-year old just swiped her boxed braids from the front of her face like I was an annoying fly. Her barrettes stung as they hit me. Then she turned over and returned to her hum.

Now she sounded like she was eating ice cream along with the cake. "Yum, yum, ... yum!"

Too excited to continue hiding, I peeked up
at the window from under the cozy quilt. And to
my surprise, twinkling eyes and a wide grin like Mama's was
playing peek-a-boo from outside the window.

Glittering from the fiery drops raining
down around her, the twinkling eyes and
shiny teeth dashed away then appeared again.

"Hey Sherry, …" I whispered. "Someone's out there."
"Mmm,mmm… yum." More curious than petrified, I slowly
peeked from under the covers at the window again.

"Peek-a-boo, I see you!" the light, laughing voice said.
I wanted to play Peek-a-boo too, but I was
too scared to move.

"Come on Chicken Little," I said aloud to myself, "you can do it!" So I counted down out loud, "five, four, three, two, one!" and bounced back up to the window.

Bravely, I smashed my face to the glass and stared at my own reflection. I could see my thin cocoa brown face and the parted hair at the top my Afro that I should have braided hours ago. Just then, a flame touched the window, followed by strangely familiar eyes.

In a flash, they ducked beneath the outside windowsill but left a huge, flaming torch hovering outside my window. Our shadows appeared in the flames on the walls of our bedroom. "Hey, come back!" I responded with a giddy laugh.

She looked so familiar, my fear quickly turned into a curious joy. I searched my brain for an old photograph to match with her face. I wondered, whose face was it?, Mama's? - Grandma D's? - Papa Jack's?

"Don't, … don't I know you?" I called out, trying to peep below the window.

She popped up sideways, still playing and giggling like a child. The torch seemed to light the sky behind her. It made her face clear.

Flexing my pointer back and forth I motioned her towards me. I made sure to grin and giggle too. Staring into the old woman's eyes, I realized they looked like mine.

"Hi Cyndi!" she said to my surprise, "Were you waiting long for me?"

"Waiting long?" I asked, "I didn't know you were coming. I was just waiting for snow."

"Hee hee hee," she laughed. "All my kinfolk wait for me. They just don't know it. Well, how do you like the 'special' snow I brought you? It's the kind of snow that only comes once every thirty years. And that's when I visit my young kin and teach 'em 'bout who they are. Tonight's your turn, little Cyndi. You ready to fly?"

"My turn? Wow! But wait. I can't go with you. I gotta go to school tomorrow."

Don't worry. You'll be back in time for school," she moved in close to my face, raised her eyebrows and said, "If there be school tomorrow."

"Okay, let's go!" I said with glee. "But, wait a minute. Where? Where are we going?"

"Somewhere special. Come!" she whispered before her head moved right through the glass window and into my room.

She peeked over at Sherry and softly
patted her head.

My new kinfolk stuck her left hand outside the window
and caught a handful of the special snowflakes and
reached for me with her right.

She sprinkled the colorful flakes over
my head, grabbed my hand and poof, like a magician's
trick we disappeared.

"COMET DUST ENVELOPED US AS WE TRAVELED BACK IN TIME, LIKE FALLING BACKWARDS INSIDE A BLACK HOLE THAT MYSTIFIED MY MIND..."

The winter storm was a sudden, distant memory. I found myself surrounded by huge southern Magnolia trees and sweating in 90-degree heat. I was still wearing my thermal pajamas.

Half walking, half running I tried to keep in step with the giant lady carrying the torch through the dark, hot woods.

"I – I think I want to go back home Miss, um Kinfolk," I said between pants. She turned with a snap; looked down at me and placed her pointer against her lips.

"Ssh. Hush chile," she said, sounding like the old ladies in church who used to live down south. I don't know why, but they say, "chile" like it's spelled with an "e" instead of 'd'.

When we arrived at a double fork in the road, she placed her finger to her lips again, pointed at a rock gesturing for me to sit then she began to dig leaves and sticks out of the ground.

" Come on Cyndi. Follow me," she said with a smile. She opened her hand for me to hold. The moment our hands touched, a sense of peace ran through me. I took in a big breath. And when the breath slowly slid back out of my nose, the sweet scents of wild flowers and peppermint were in the air.

The entrance had just enough space for her thin frame. "Come on Cyndi." I follwed and turned the corner to find a huge underground shelter, bigger than Mama and Daddy's master bedroom.

"Wow. What a cool hideout. It's just like Batman's!" I admitted to my new friend adorned in her patchwork handmade dress. The temperature was cool too.

"You look pretty, ma'am? Um sorry, I don't know your name. What should I call you?"

"Folk call me Elsie here but
my real name is Mama Adenrele.
Ah – Den – Relly she pronounced it for me to repeat.

"Ah-den-relly," I repeated as she placed the upside down
torch inside a makeshift furnace in the middle of the cave.

"It rhymes with jelly!" I said and looked up to see if her big
grin was still there. I hoped she thought my joke was
funny. It was and she did. Her head had fallen back and a
giant laugh roared up from her belly.

"That's a good one Cyndi," she said as she rubbed her belly
with one hand and my head with the other, "You can call
me Mama Relly, who rhymes with Jelly!"

"It's a Yoruba name, Cyndi." Mama Relly explained.

"Hmm, that's interesting," I tried to sound serious too. "I'm in the third grade. This year we learned about Yoruba people in school. They are from West Africa," I said proudly.

"That's right chile; we are!" She replied with a quick nod like she was impressed. I cheesed some more.

Then Mama Relly sat on an old wooden stool I'm guessing she made herself and pointed to the one in front of her. I obeyed. The former tree trunks were covered with mini patchwork quilts filled with bunches of rags and much more comfortable than I expected.

"**I FELT LIKE LITTLE RED RIDING HOOD HIDING IN THE WOODS, BUT THE WOLVES HERE WERE WHITE MEN WITH ROPES AND BIG HOODS...**"

There were four more placed throughout the windowless circular room – each in every direction. The blue one was north. Pretty as the sky, it was placed next to the water-filled pail for washing. East set another stool, yellow like sunrise. Covered in beads, it was near the red and white quilted pallet. It was close to the small fire that kept the room dimly lit.

The Southerm stool had a thinner cover. It was coupled with a big wooden spoon. Next to it was an ancient pestle and mortar set, a small spoon and a meal bowl covered with a white cloth. The West stool set before a plugged hole and a long tube. Dried flowers were above each stool and lined the entryway. We sat in the center.

"Mama Relly? Why do you live in a cave?
And why did you bring me here?"

Her smile vanished. Her lips got tight as memories of terror caused her big eyes to stretch wider, "Cyndi, I must live here. You see, I been hiding from the slave catchers for years. I was a slave once but I will not let them make me a slave again."

"What! This is slavery time?
You have to take me back home right now.
I can't stay here Mama Relly," I ranted in a panic.

"Don't fret chile. No one can bother you here. No one!
But I do need you to promise to help me before I take
you back home."

"Sure," I promised. "What do you need me to do?"
"I want to go back home. Home to Africa!" she yelled
with excitement. "That is why my Papa named me,
Adenrelle, Ade means The crown and Relle means
returns to the throne; 'the crown returns home.' I've
tried and tried but never made it home."

"That is so sad, Mama Relly," I said with a frown.

"Cyndi, I'm a need you to go home for me."
"I'm only eight; how can I go to Africa in your place?" I
asked with eyebrows like question marks.
She smiled and shook her head.

"No little one. It won't work that way.
You don't have to leave today chile but
you can replace me. You know why?" she asked.

"Why?" I screamed with excitement, not knowing what she
could possibly say next.

"Well, I'm your ancestor, that's why. You remember your
Grandma Jesse you used to visit in North Carolina?" she
asked as she ignored how my hands quickly covered my open
mouth. "You know my Grandma Jesse?"

"She's only my first grandchild," she said with pride.
She continued to explain as I stared in her face still unable
to close my mouth. I couldn't say another word. In my head I
was counting the generations to
figure out how many "greats" should go before
Mama Relly's name.

"My great-great-great grandma
or at least I think. She's worth more
than gold or fur coats of mink,
I must be dreaming, this just can't be true,
I wonder if I could have made it

if I was a slave too..."

"You really are my ancestor!" I squealed, jumped up and hugged her neck as hard as I could. "I knew it. Something told me we were related. I always wanted to meet my ancestors. This is amazing!" I screamed with joyous tears flowing down my face.

"Whoa! She yelled in shock, not expecting my response. At first she was unable to respond. Untouched by love for so long she kinda froze. Unable to resist, seconds later she re-signed, wrapped her arms around me and squeezed tight like her love was longing to be received for a lifetime.

"Listen Cyndi," she spoke softly and kissed my cheek as I sat, "we only have a little time together now but if you want, I will come and get you from time to time. And, we's can plan your trip back to Africa."

"I SAT BACK AND SUDDENLY THE HIDEOUT TOOK ON A BRIGHTER SHADE, LIKE IT'S WHERE A BIT OF HEAVEN HAS BEEN SAVED...

I STARTED SEEING VISIONS OF HER AND A CHEROKEE MAN MOVING ABOUT THE CAVE. MAYBE HE'S THE FOUR GREATS GRANDPA THAT MADE HER BRAVE."

As she talked about Africa, Mama Relly walked over to the semi-circle and uncovered the bowl. She took food out and flattened it into patties.

She swiftly grabbed the square white salt rock from over the furnace, placed the food on the salt block then placed the salt block on the fire like she'd done it a million times.

"You hungry chile?" she asked without looking and somehow knowing what I'd say.

"Yes ma'am," I said, remembering my manners. "Can I ask you something Mama Relly?"

"Go'on chile. What you wanna know?"

"Does your husband still live here too?"

Silently she smiled then froze like a statue.
She spoke soft and slow.

"He was gonna take me back you know. Take
me back to Africa. A great man was he.
Great man." She repeated. "Great man."

Then Mama Relly told me all about
her husband– 'Day'.

"Dega-taga was his name,
but I called him Day.
It always made him laugh out loud
when I said his name that way...

He snatched me from a hungry bear, my first
night in the woods,
and gave me his torch to scare animals away,
so I knew that he was good...

We bonded that night like we had known one
another for years,
I guess I made him feel important
and he took away all my fears...

Like a married couple, we made a pact for life.

And though we were only nine years old,
we knew we'd be man and wife."

"Wow. I wish I could've met him," I said with a sigh. You know what Mama Relly? I would love to come and see you again but I don't think Mama and Papa will allow it."

"Don't you fret," she said as she flipped the corn patties, "they will never know. You will see."

"As long as I don't end up getting a whipping, I'm in," I responded without batting an eye.

"What? They whoop you? Don't they know better than whooping a chile! Bad 'nough we have to get whooped by the master and anybody else who sees fit," she almost burned herself removing the hot food with her bare fingers. Mama Relly shook with fury and darted her eyes at me, "You got scars chile?"

"No, no ma'am. Wait, you don't understand. It's not really a whipping," I tried to explain, "just a spanking, and it was only one time. And they don't really use a whip," I half smiled as I pleaded for understanding.

"I don't even know why we used that word, "whipping … ," I whispered at the end, but she had gotten so mad, I didn't think she could even hear me anymore. A fuse that lived within the belly of her pain had been lit.

"Well, … I know why they calls it that. It's 'cause we used to get whipped with a real whip. But they can't whip ME no more. Can't none of 'em find me here!"

"Yes ma'am," I whispered and hung my head.

"That's why I ran off back in '33?" Mama Relly's head spun around with a snap. "Wanna know how I escaped?" she asked and winked.

"You ran away from home in 1933?" I asked foolishly.

"No chile. I escaped from slavery back in 1833."

"Wow! Of course I wanna know!" I quickly responded.

"How did you do it?" I asked anxiously.

Mama Relly sat across me on the north stool. I sat to the east. She exhaled like she was getting rid of all the anger she felt a minute before and started with a long, "Well, ... it was a strange November night in Virginny on the Walker Plantation. That where I was a slave. I remember 'cause it was chilly. I was just a little girl 'bout your age more or less. Just setting out front, list'nin to folk talk 'fore goin' to bed.

"This here is a snow sky," said Big Larry, the oldest Black man on the place. He was looking up with his arm stretched up at the night sky. So we all looked up too.

"Mm hm. Sho is," everyone agreed. The sky was filling up fast with white flurries that grew bigger and bigger by the second. Then, they swirled in a huge circle and started pouring down out the sky. And soon as they hit the ground, they turned into red, blue and yellow sparks."
"Like the ones I saw!" I added.

"That's right chile. Well, … What kind a snow is this?" folk
started asking. Some started jumping and running 'cause
the "special snow" was turning into little fires
as it hit the ground.

But not me. I wasn't scared at all. I thought to myself,
this is a sign. "Signs always come when you need to make
a move." That's what my mama used to say.

Big Larry ran to tell Master Walker that stars was falling out the sky. Soon as Master Walker came out on the big house porch, he looked up and shouted, "Lord have mercy on my soul!" Then he hollered at the top of his lungs,

"Y'ALL COME 'ROUND HERE! RUN, FAST AS Y'ALL CAN! IT'S THE END OF THE WORLD!"

"Master Walker was usually mean. He was the opposite of Santa Claus: skinny, mean and took instead of giving. But that night, he looked scared. And for the first time, he wasn't mad. He talked real fast, like he was running out of time."

"Well, y'all know that I'm a Christian man."
"Yes, sir," we all kinda mumbled not knowing what to expect. "And from the look of that there sky, seems to me, ..." he hung his head and placed his hat over his heart as he continued, "the good Lord's about to call us all home!"

We all froze in shock as he rattled on,
"I know in my heart that it's wrong to make anyone a
slave and I been mean to y'all. But when I sold your
folks off, it was just business to me. And, … I'm – uh
sorry and I never meant to hurt y'all."

Like statues with open mouths, we listened closely.
"So's I can be right with the Lord 'fore I die," he continued, "I'm a tell all y'all where your kinfolk live."

Well, … it was 50 or so of us. Happy and scared, we all
stood under the falling fiery stars as he went down his
long list, talking like an auctioneer. He told every child
where they ma and pa was and every ma and pa where
their child was. Folk cried with joy to finally know their
kin was still alive. Then they ran as fast as they could.
Finally I heard him say my name.

" 'Lil' Elsie, you know your Pa died running off. He's buried in the back fields. I sold your Ma to Mr. Wendell Brown that next day,' he rattled off in a half second without a care. "The Brown Plantation be just 5 miles north of here," he added and pointed at the big iron gate at the entrance of the plantation as if he expected me to take off that very second.

"Well Cyndi, I knew what I had to do. You see, I'm a runner just like my Pa was. He was so fast that he used to take messages to villages 10 miles away when we lived in Africa. So I didn't need to hear another word. I took off like lightning the moment he said, 'north' but first, I ran to the quarters near the kitchen where I slept and grabbed my pallet. I stuffed my few rags of clothes inside it, tied it round a stick and ran right out that gate.

"I heard tales of the slave catchers who snatched up anybody Black, slave or free. So I hid behind every big tree I could when I needed to catch my breath. Cold, happy and scared to death, I ran for hours through that storm. I figured if I'm a die, I wanna die in my mama's arms."

"I COULD SEE HER AS A LITTLE GIRL,
RUNNING IN THE SNOW.
COULD I EVER BE THAT BRAVE?
I GUESS I'LL NEVER KNOW."

Mama Relly stopped for a second. She had jumped
to her feet and her arms were flingiing back and
forth like she was running for her life.

Her eyes were looking right through me, like she saw
something behind me that would save her life if she
could just get to it. Then all at once, she stopped.

She sat back down on her stool and sighed.

"You know what Cyndi? I never did find the Brown Plantation or my mama. I got so tired from running that I laid down right in front of that tree outside this cave and fell fast asleep. And when I woke up ,the stars had stopped falling, the world had kept turning and I was free!"

"Wow! Did you hide here for the rest of your life?"

"Pretty much. I took care of myself for a little while too. 'Fore God sent me an angel. Your great-great-great grand daddy. Wouldn't a survived with out him! He even helped me looked for my mama."

She knew I saw her face change and turned away. Her head dropped and I knew Mama Relly was crying. Seeing her so upset made me cry too. So, I tried to think of something that would make her smile.

"Dont cry, Mama Jelly," I said with a big silly grin. "I mean, Relly!" She looked at me then gently lifted my chin with her hand.

"I like you Cyndi, you reminde me of myself as a chile— always happy and joking. Don't ever lose your joy."

"I won't Mama Relly. I like you too. You outsmarted those slave catchers and you came all the way to Brooklyn to find me. I'll stay with you a while if it will make you happy."

For a minute I thought I could get used to living in the south with Mama Relly even though I still didn't know how I got here. If I did, I could find out more about her "peoples" - my people. She would have time to tell me how she got back here and how she found me.

"Come here chile." She pulled me closer and onto her lap. I happily hopped aboard. "Yes Mama Relly?"

"I need you to promise me, you goin' back to Africa one day. If you gonna do it, say Sankofa!"

"Sankofa!" I repeated.

"That means, "Return to home and remember who we be," her brown eyes looked deep into mine and I could hear her heartbeat. Our hearts beat like we were one.

"I promise Mama Relly, I promise. What was that word again?"

"Sankofa. It means go back and 'member who you be," she accented each word with a light poke in my belly.

"Sankofa," I repeat. "Remember who I be - African."

"Good girl Cyndi. I knew you were the one." She smiled, tilted her head and handed me the corn cake, "Now, eat little one."

I smiled and tilted my head too, "Thank you Mama Relly. Mm, … this is good."

We smiled between each chew and the heartbeat got louder. I felt so comfortable; I fell fast asleep chewing my last corncake bite and hugging Mama Relly.

"CORNCAKE CRUMBS FILL THE
CORNERS OF MY SMILE,
LEANING BACK I FELT LIKE HER CHILD.
LIKE A COMFORTER, HER ARMS WRAPPED ME
IN A FOLD; HER HEARTBEAT'S A LULLABY
OF STORIES ANCESTORS ONCE TOLD..."

"Cyndi! Girl have you been in that window all night?"
Mama fussed as she peeled my face off the bay window.

"I guess you already know nobody's going to school with
all that snow out there. Eighteen inches. My Lord. How
am I gonna get to work today? Come child, Let me help
you in the bed."

"Mama Relly?" I asked as Mama lifted me up and walked over to my bed. "No, just Mama," she said. I felt her moist lips kissing my forehead.

"Rest chile; you couldn't have slept well on that windowsill."

"Really Cyndi, I don't know what is in that head of yours sometimes," Mama pretended to check my head for a fever.

"Mama?" I remember asking.

"Yes Cyndi?" she patiently responded.

"Can we go to Africa?" I asked before falling back asleep in her arms.

"Africa? Hm. I don't see why not," she whispered. "Gotta keep our word to Mama Relly, don't we?"

Then she looked back at the window and said, "One day Mama Relly. One day."

THE AUTHOR AND ILLUSTRATOR

Cathie Wright-Lewis is the author of Maurya's Seed, Passion's Pride and Afro-futuristic Literature for Learning, Exodus 2055 and Mama Relly found on iTunes.

She is a retired high school teacher from Brooklyn who creates tools for learning African American history and Literacy Analysis.

See more of her current and future work at www.cathiewrightlewis.com

Cheyenne "Angel" Lewis is a digital and traditional artist. She is the illustrator, Cover and Book Designer for Mama Relly as well as the cover artist for Passion's Pride.

She is a recent college graduate from Bowie State University and resides in New York City to start her career as an artist.

See Examples of her work at www.cosmicxfuse.tumblr.com